ADDIS
BERNER BEAR
FORGETS

For London and the people who
have lent it to me.
J.S.

ADDIS BERNER BEAR FORGETS
A PICTURE CORGI BOOK 978 0 552 55434 3

First published in Great Britain by Doubleday,
an imprint of Random House Children's Books
A Random House Group Company

Doubleday edition published 2008
Picture Corgi edition published 2008

1 3 5 7 9 10 8 6 4 2

Picture Corgi Books are published by Random House Children's Books,
61–63 Uxbridge Road, London W5 5SA

www.**kids**at**randomhouse**.co.uk
www.**rbooks**.co.uk

Addresses for companies within The Random House Group Limited can be found at:
www.randomhouse.co.uk/offices.htm

THE RANDOM HOUSE GROUP Limited Reg. No. 954009

A CIP catalogue record for this book is available from the British Library.

Printed in Singapore

ADDIS BERNER BEAR FORGETS

JOEL STEWART

PICTURE CORGI

When Addis Berner Bear came
to the city it was winter.

It was so big and confusing,

so loud and fast,

that he forgot everything that he had left behind.

But he forgot why he had come, too.

Addis found his way a little,

spoke to the people who would speak to him,

and sheltered where he could.

Time and a lot of things went by.

Some made his heart leap,

some made his fur bristle,

some made him cross-eyed.

It was all so much, and still
Addis Berner Bear couldn't remember
why he had come to the city.

He wasn't the only one.

Then something terrible happened.

And something amazing!

Addis Berner Bear remembered why he had come
to the city. He was top of the bill!

But how in the world could he play
for everyone without his trumpet?

Addis Berner Bear played.

The music was big and confusing,
loud and fast.

It was heart-leaping,

fur-bristling,

cross-eye making

. . . and beautiful.

It was a day that Addis Berner Bear
would never forget.